Emily's Perfect Pet!

Jonathan Shipton
Garry Parsons

GULLANE
CHILDREN'S BOOKS

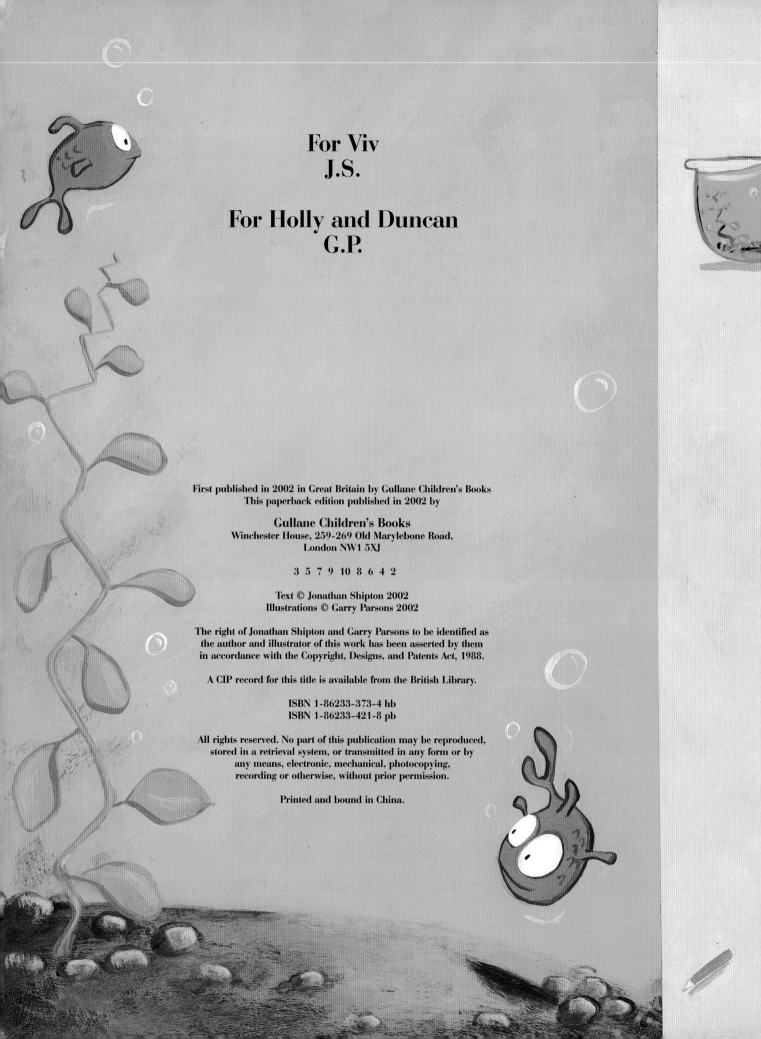

For Viv
J.S.

For Holly and Duncan
G.P.

First published in 2002 in Great Britain by Gullane Children's Books
This paperback edition published in 2002 by

Gullane Children's Books
Winchester House, 259-269 Old Marylebone Road,
London NW1 5XJ

3 5 7 9 10 8 6 4 2

Text © Jonathan Shipton 2002
Illustrations © Garry Parsons 2002

The right of Jonathan Shipton and Garry Parsons to be identified as
the author and illustrator of this work has been asserted by them
in accordance with the Copyright, Designs, and Patents Act, 1988.

A CIP record for this title is available from the British Library.

ISBN 1-86233-373-4 hb
ISBN 1-86233-421-8 pb

Printed and bound in China.

Emily's Perfect Pet!

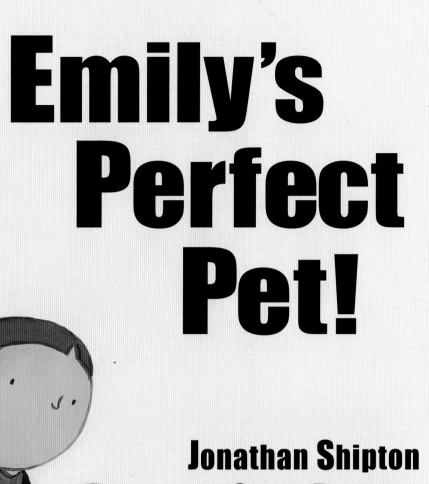

Jonathan Shipton
Garry Parsons

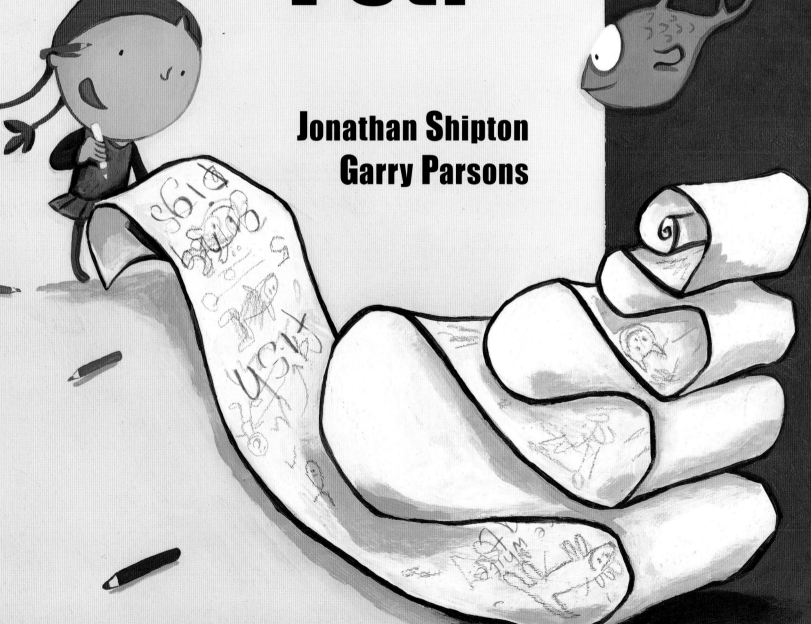

It was Emily's birthday
and she wanted a pet.
Emily had always wanted a pet.
But Emily's mum said:
"Pets are a lot of hard work."
And Emily's dad agreed.
"Two legs good," he said.
"Four legs bad."

Emily went off
to school looking
quite sad.

When Emily came home from school,
she had made a list.
It was called "My Pets".
At the top of the list was "**ponies**".
Emily read out all the good things about ponies.
And when she'd finished, Emily's mum said:
"The trouble is . . .

Ponies cost an awful
lot to feed.
And they need a stable.
And a field.
And . . .
You have to clean them out,
and groom them
Every Single Day!"

And Emily's dad said, he had a pony once.

And it **kicked!**

So Emily crossed
ponies off the list.

"What about a **puppy**?" Emily said.

"Puppies don't need fields.

Puppies just need sticks…
And tickling…
And chasing around the garden."

But Emily's
mum said…

"I expect there would be dog hair. Everywhere.
And muddy paw prints on the carpet."

And Emily's dad said:
"I had a puppy once . . .
And it grew into a huge
slobbery dog with great
big feet that dug
enormous
holes in the grass.

"Oh," said Emily and crossed puppies off her list.

So Emily told them all about **kittens**.
She told them about the stripy fur . . .
And the little pink noses . . .
And the soft blue eyes . . .
She told them about all the brilliant
games you could play with a piece
of string and a fluffy kitten.

Emily's dad shook
his head and said . . .

"But the trouble is . . .
Small fluffy kittens turn into big mangy cats
that have terrible breath . . .
And they make messes in the garden . . .
And they have *fleas*."

So that was that. For cats.

"What about a nice white **rat**?"
suggested Emily.
"They don't bark,
they don't claw the furniture,
they don't need a stable.
Rats are very intelligent!"
said Emily.

And Emily's
dad said . . .

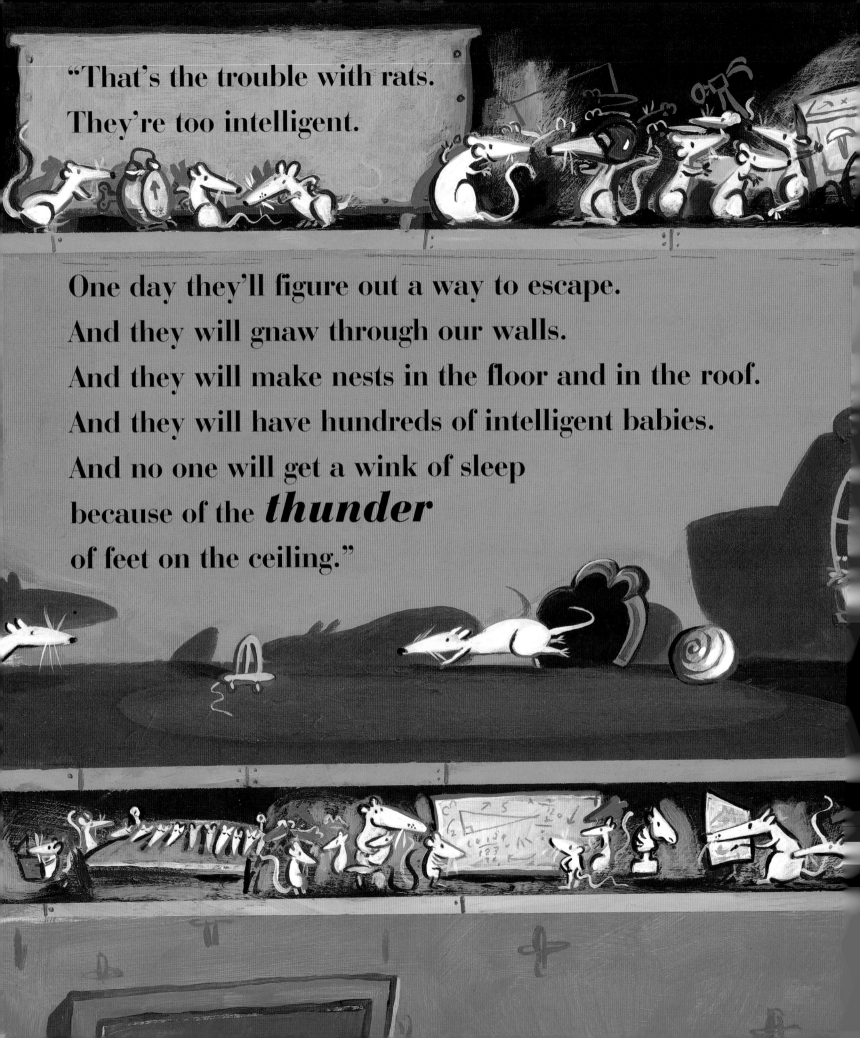

"That's the trouble with rats.
They're too intelligent.

One day they'll figure out a way to escape.
And they will gnaw through our walls.
And they will make nests in the floor and in the roof.
And they will have hundreds of intelligent babies.
And no one will get a wink of sleep
because of the *thunder*
of feet on the ceiling."

And Emily's mum didn't say anything.
But she shivered.

Emily moved down the list to **fish**.
"Six good things about goldfish,"
said Emily quietly.
"**1.** You can decorate their
bowls with stones and
mermaids and things.

2. They don't make much
noise so you can have
them in your room.

3. They don't cost much.

4. They don't dig up the garden.

5. They don't bite or scratch or kick.

6. They just swim."

"Exactly!" said Emily's dad. "That's the annoying thing about goldfish. They just go around and around *Not Doing Anything!*"

Emily looked down at her list and sighed.

"Last but not least," she said,

"are . . . **Guinea Pigs**.

They're not too small and not too big.

And they're not too clever. And they're not too stupid.

And sometimes they get so happy, they make little squeaks.

And they wouldn't even want to escape, because . . .

I would play with them Every Day.

And stroke them Every Day.

And fill up their water Every Day."

Emily's mum didn't say a word.
And Emily's dad wasn't
even listening...

Emily tore her list into little bits.
Then she stomped out
into the garden, where . . .

...Emily's dad was standing.

Snuggled in his jumper was something not too small
and not too big, not too clever and not too stupid,
something very soft and furry with a round bottom.

Something that made
little happy squeaks.